Acknowledgment

I would like to acknowledgment my dear friend, Dawn Andres, for her exceptional editing skills and unwavering support throughout the process of my children's book. Dawn's friendship and encouragement have been invaluable in this journey. I am grateful for her contribution, and I highly recommend her to anyone seeking a talented editor and a wonderful friend. Thank you, Dawn.

I would like to dedicate a special acknowledgment to my older sister and Co Author, Fatima. Despite the challenges posed by Multiple Sclerosis, you have shown immense strength, resilience, and determination. It was during our high school years that we first collaborated on the creation of the enchanting children's story, "Little Dipper and Luna." Your unwavering support, creative input, and boundless love have been instrumental in shaping the story into something truly special. I am eternally grateful for your inspiration and the cherished memories we have shared throughout this journey. Thank you, dear sister, for the immeasurable impact you have had on my life. I love you deeply, and I am forever thankful for you.

I would like to acknowledge my talented illustrator/ niece, Sierra, who has brought my book to life with her incredible illustrations. Sierra, your creative mind and artistic skills are truly mesmerizing and will captivate readers of all ages. Your illustrations have added a whole new dimension to the story, enchanting the minds of those who immerse themselves in its pages. I am grateful for the dedication and passion you have poured into it. Thank you, Sierra, for sharing your remarkable talent and for bringing my words to life. Your contribution to this book is immeasurable.

Little Dipper & Luna

I am Bright Enough!

This Book Belongs to:

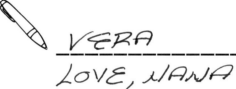

VERA

_____

LOVE, NANA

Once upon a time in a galaxy far, far away lived a star named Little Dipper.

His best friend, Luna, a crescent moon, lived there too.

Little Dipper loved to play with Luna every day. But today he didn't feel like playing.

"Oh no! Why is my friend so sad?" said Luna. She didn't know what to do!

After some time, Luna came by to ask again, "Little Dipper, do you want to play in Milky Way Park?" He shook his head no.

Milky Way Park

He would rather sit in his room feeling sorry for himself. "I'll never shine as brightly as the other stars in the sky" he thought.

Suddenly, an idea came to him. "I need some shiny lights, then my glow would be brighter!"

Off he went to find some old Christmas lights. But where can they be?
He remembered the big brown box.

Yes! Here they are!
He lit up the room like a tree on
Christmas day!

But still, it was not bright enough for Little Dipper. Even these lights can't make me shine, he thought. He felt so silly.

Then, Little Dipper had another idea - a brilliant idea!

"Yes! This will do the trick!"

He ran to his arts and crafts closet to get his jug of glitter!

15

Little Dipper filled the tub with water, poured in the glitter, and jumped in!

He splashed and splashed until there was glitter everywhere—everywhere but on Little Dipper. It wasn't sticking to him!

"I'll never shine brightly, not ever," he thought.

He dried off and noticed a bottle of lotion on the sink. It read "Shimmery lotion to boost glow." That's it! This just had to work!

19

He used the whole bottle.
"Now I smell like vanilla pudding", he thought. But still, there was no shine.

Little Dipper had lost all hope.

21

Luna was not giving up on her friend, so
she went to see him again.
Moon pies and chocolate pudding would
surely cheer him.

These are his favorites!

When the door opened, Little Dipper was crying. Luna hugged her best friend. "Are you okay?"

"Tell me why you've been sad?"

Little Dipper wiped his tears. "I don't shine as brightly as the other stars," he said.

Luna could not believe it! Why would he want to be like the others?

Didn't he know how special he was? To her, he is the brightest star in the galaxy!

27

After all, he was the best friend anyone could ask for. He was smart and caring and had a spirit that shined brighter than the sun.

29

30

"You're right!" he shouted.
Thank you, Luna!

**"I am bright enough!
I am special just the way I am."**

32

Sometimes friends just need to be told how special they are, share Moon Pies and pudding, and go play in Milky Way Park.

Little Dipper realized that his brightness didn't come from things like Christmas lights or glitter, but from the love and support of his best friend Luna.

35

✦ **A testament to the unbreakable bond of two sisters** ✦
and the power of their storytelling.

Made in the USA
Columbia, SC
13 October 2024